RECIPIENT:

Potential Special Agent,
Human Division

WITHDRAWN

If you have found this book, it is no accident. Our agents have been working to get this into your hands for a very long time now.

You are holding official declassified materials from THE FANTASTIC BUREAU OF IMAGINATION. This story is true. However, portions have been changed to protect the figment (or figments) involved.

More agents of imagination are needed! Your compassion and creativity would be a vital addition to our team. We hope you will read and join us.

Should you choose not to join our ranks, we have placed a large bear outside of your home. (He is invisible.) We assure you he does not bite, but he does like to ramble on and on about incredibly boring things. So, it is in your best interest to do the right thing.

Warm regards,

Agent Whim

Recruitment and special projects division

P.S. OK! OK! I was kidding about the bear thing. We just really want y̶ an agent. Please consider.

F O R   C O R R E Y

DIAL BOOKS FOR YOUNG READERS
An imprint of Penguin Random House LLC, New York

First published in the United States of America by Dial Books for Young Readers,
an imprint of Penguin Random House LLC, 2023

Text copyright © 2023 by Brad Montague
Pictures copyright © 2023 by Brad Montague and Kristi Montague

Visit us online at penguinrandomhouse.com.

Library of Congress Cataloging-in-Publication Data is available.

Manufactured in Italy

ISBN 9780593323472

1 3 5 7 9 10 8 6 4 2

LEG

Design by Cerise Steel
Text set in GeoSlab

The artwork for this book was created using real and imaginary textures. Pencil on paper,
colored and collaged together using Procreate.

The agents of the Fantastic Bureau of Imagination wish to thank all humans who have
taken time to help this story be told. Some figment names have been changed, but some
have not been changed. This was done to keep you on your toes.

Every song that has ever been sung,

Every piece of art that has ever been hung,

Every dream that's ever been dreamed,

They all began in a place not so easily seen . . .

WORDS BY
BRAD MONTAGUE

PICTURES BY
BRAD and KRISTI
MONTAGUE

 Dial Books for Young Readers

Welcome to the Fantastic Bureau of Imagination.

Apologies, but humans are not allowed to
see the outside of our secret headquarters.
It is highly classified.
You'll just have to imagine it.

Some young humans have mailed us art to show what they think our building looks like.

TiNY.
dooR
ON THe
mooN

• Exhibit #7805 •

• Exhibit #0621 •

Dear figmenta,

• Exhibit #1999 •

• Exhibit #7572 •

Most of our agency business is handled by
curious little creatures known as figments.

FIELD FIGMENT   LIGHT FIGMENT   ELDER FIGMENT   GARDEN FIGMENT

WATER FIGMENT   FIRE FIGMENT   FOREST FIGMENT   MUSIC FIGMENT

FASHION FIGMENT   FORGING FIGMENT   INVISIBLE FIGMENT   MERFIGMENT

PIGMENT FIGMENT   WISH FIGMENT   SEED FIGMENT   ROCK FIGMENT

Every figment you'll meet here is a special agent and
carries a very official Bureau of Imagination badge.

This is Sparky. He's the figment responsible for all our mail here. Every letter, package, idea, or complaint coming in or out of the Fantastic Bureau of Imagination must pass through his office.

As you can imagine, he is a very busy little figment.
He is also very good at his job. But there is something the agents here do not know about him . . .

Sparky loves to write poetry.

When not delivering the mail, he writes poems about brave
figments throughout history.
He writes about his dear friend Rascal the dreampuppy.
He writes about all the big feelings inside of him.

He writes poems about how scary it would be
to share his poems.

You see, Sparky has never shared his writing with
any figment (or human, gnome, dragon, or bug) ever.
Instead, he throws himself into his very big job.

Life is busy for Sparky.

He always starts the day by going down the official tubes,

WHOOSH!

through the whoosh-scalator,

over the Cave of Untold Stories past Brenda (she never gets mail),

and makes delivery after delivery to agents
throughout the Fantastic Bureau of Imagination.

The figments at the Department of Dreams are always excited to see Sparky. His magic mailbag can carry dreams of all sizes.

The figments cheer anytime he delivers new equipment to the Department of Noticing. These agents listen for wishes as they're made on birthday cakes, dandelions, or stars in the sky.

Ideas from all over the world are delivered to The Makery. The figments in this office can experiment and create samples of anything that can be imagined. One of Sparky's favorite days was when the agents created a plant that grew Popsicles, a flying 1980s station wagon, and a rabbit with a beautiful singing voice.

Sparky never leaves The Makery without making a
pickle sandwich. (Busy figments need to eat.)

Once all the mail is sorted, stacked, and delivered to each of the Bureau offices . . .

THE FANTASTIC BUREAU OF IMAGINATION
(a few rooms we're allowed to show you)

1. Hall of History
2. Secret Entrance
3. Classified Storage
4. Office of Interest
5. Dept. of Doodles
6. Dreampuppy Offices
7. Agents of Awe
8. Office of Frightening Things
9. Taste Task Force
10. Build-A-Beast Workshop
11. Library of Everything

12. Planetarium of Possibility
13. Idea Lab
14. Infinite Hallway (access to all other offices from here)
15. Dept. of Repaired and Reimagined Things
16. Office of Optimism
17. Dept. of Color
18. Dept. of Connecting
19. Junior Figment Training
20. Dept. of Dreams
21. Dept. of Music

22. Whoosh-scalator Waiting Area 2
23. Misfiled Ideas
24. Wish Team Six
25. Dept. of Wonder
26. Tube to Dept. of Noticing
27. Office of Celebrations
28. Lost and Found
29. Tree of Stories
30. Sea of Searching
31. Forging Figment
32. Cave of Untold Stories

Sparky sits, enjoys his sandwich, and writes a poem.
At least, this is what Sparky did every single day at the
Fantastic Bureau of Imagination . . . until today . . .

Today, Sparky went down the official tubes,

WHOOSH!

through the whoosh-scalator,

Sparky froze. He had never spoken to Brenda.
Each day, he'd been secretly relieved that she did not receive
mail. He was frightened by her teeth and scales.

He imagined she might eat him

or laugh at his hat

or laugh while eating him and his hat.

Though very much afraid, he knew something had to be done.
Surprising Rascal—and even himself—Sparky dove down to help.

"The Cave of Untold Stories is overflowing!" cried Brenda.
"The entire Bureau of Imagination could collapse!"

All the stories that have yet to be told in the world, all the songs that have not yet been sung, all the parties yet to be planned, and all the problems yet to be solved . . . they were all pouring out.

"If only there were a way to let humans know," said the troubled dragon. "Ideas are not just meant for having and holding, but for sharing and living and doing."

Sparky tried to put some of the cave pieces in his official Bureau mailbag. (Being a magic bag, it was able to hold more than most bags, but even it was not enough.)

He looked at all the wonderful things that'd been imagined—

Beautiful symphonies . . .

performances and plays . . .

marvelous inventions . . .

ideas for brightening days.

All these wonders were just hiding away in a cave.

As Sparky gazed at the mess, his eyes noticed something familiar. Mixed in the pile of possibilities was a large stack of poems he recognized immediately.

"Oh no," he said. "Part of the problem is me."

He flew to his office and quickly began to write:

Hello humans!
We need you to be BOLD.
There are too many stories
that remain UNTOLD!
There's still so many good things
and they haven't been done.
AGENTS of IMAGINATION are needed
and YOU CAN BE ONE!

This is your invitation.
Tell fear to get out of the way.
BEAUTIFUL TOMORROWS CAN BEGIN TODAY!

We must all dare to DREAM,
but must also DO!
For dreamers are many,
but doers are few.

imaginatively yours,

SPARKY

OFFICIAL MAIL FIGMENT,
FANTASTIC BUREAU of IMAGINATION

This poem did not go in Sparky's
stack of hidden notebooks . . .

Soon untold stories were finally being shared.
Songs were being sung and dances were danced. Problems
were being solved and the cave began to calm.

Everyone gathered to celebrate three brave agents: a dragon, a dreampuppy, and a little mail figment. The heroes were each presented with the highest medal of honor an agent can receive. Their work had added more imagination to the world and more agents of imagination too.

They all lived happily and imaginatively ever after, until . . .

Brenda ate Sparky.

Just kidding.

daily poem #077 for Brenda

We imagined things we couldn't see.
We worked together and made them be!
Maybe this is how the whole world mends:
Wherever there is fear,
LET US IMAGINE FRIENDS!

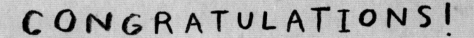

CONGRATULATIONS!

You have been chosen to join the ranks
of the Fantastic Bureau of Imagination.

STEP ONE:
CREATE a BADGE

Using whatever resources
are available to you
(paper, cardboard,
lettuce, whatever!), design
your official Agent of
Imagination badge.
Wear it with pride.